THIS BOOK BELONGS TO

_____

_____

A LITTLE OWL BOOK

TOM THUMB

retold by Hilda Young
illustrated by Jo Berriman

WORLD

There was once a poor woodcutter and his wife who were very sad because they had no children.

"I should be happy with one child, even though he was only as big as my thumb," sighed the woodcutter's wife.

"Yes, indeed, we should love him dearly," agreed her husband.

And great was their joy when a child was born to them some time later.

Although he was strong and healthy, with a ready wit and a merry tongue, the boy never grew any bigger than his father's thumb, and for this reason he was called Tom Thumb.

But his parents loved him dearly and his mother made him a hat from an oak leaf, a silk shirt, a jacket of thistledown and soft leather trousers and shoes.

One day Tom's father went off to cut some logs, leaving Tom to drive the donkey cart. How did such a small little fellow do this? Why, his mother placed Tom in the donkey's ear, and Tom told the animal which way to go! Tom might be small, but he was also very clever!

Tom passed two men who were most surprised to see a cart driven by a carter they could hear but not see. They followed the cart into the wood and they were amazed to see Tom climb out of the donkey's ear.

"This boy could make our fortune," they cried.

Tom persuaded his father to accept the gold coins that the two men offered in exchange for Tom. "Don't worry, Father, I shall soon be back home again," he whispered.

So the two men set off to the next town, Tom travelling on the broad brim of one of the men's hats.

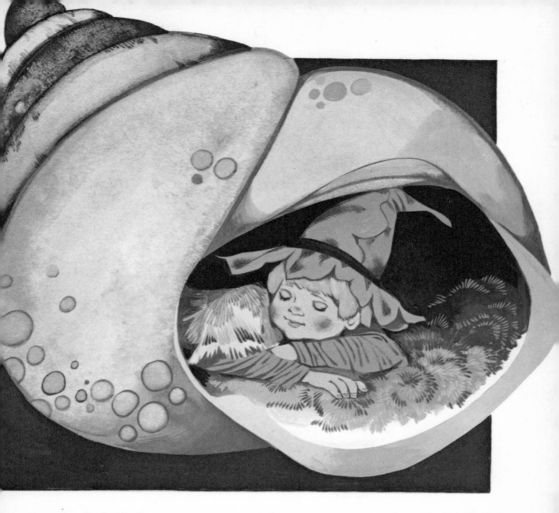

As dusk fell the men stopped to rest in a ploughed field. Tom jumped down from the hat and hid in an old mousehole, refusing to come out until the men went on their way.

Then he crept into an empty snail shell lined with soft moss and slept sweetly until daybreak.

Tom now intended to return home, but alas for his hopes!
As he walked along the highway, a raven swooped down
and picked up poor Tom. The raven flew with Tom over the
sea . . . and dropped the little man in the waves!

A large fish caught Tom in its mouth and swallowed him. "What a pretty pickle!" cried Tom as he gazed around him. But good fortune was with him, for the fish was caught and taken to the royal palace as a gift for the king.

What a surprise the cook got when she opened up the fish to cook it, and out popped Tom! But when she had recovered her senses, she washed Tom in a large cup of soapy water, dried him out, and took him along to see the king.

The king and queen were delighted to see such a handsome
little fellow. They ordered the royal tailor to make Tom a fine
satin suit and the royal hatmaker made him an elegant cap
with a feather.

Tom soon became a firm favourite at court. He was always taken on a royal hunt, sitting in front of the king on the best horse in the royal stables. Even when it chanced to rain during the hunt Tom never got wet. He would creep into the king's waistcoat pocket and stay there, snug and dry, until the rain stopped!

Tom also spent some time each day amusing the queen and her ladies. They would sit together in the royal gardens listening to the royal musicians play. Sometimes Tom would sing the queen a little song, for he had a very sweet voice.

But sometimes Tom could be rather naughty! One day he was playing cherry stones with Crispin when the royal page noticed that although Tom was losing, the little man still had lots of stones. He was creeping inside Crispin's cherry stone bag and stealing stones when he thought Crispin wasn't looking!

So Crispin decided to teach Tom a lesson! He waited until Tom had climbed into the bag once more, and then he drew the bag strings tightly together. Then Crispin gave the bag a great big shake! Poor Tom! His legs and shoulders were so badly bruised that he promised never to cheat at games again!

Tom often talked to the king about his parents. One day the king suggested that Tom should return home to show his mother and father that he was alive and well.

"Take them some money as a gift from me," added the king. So Tom went down to the royal treasury and put a large gold coin in his purse.

Tom heaved his heavy purse upon his back and he started off for home. He travelled all that day and all the next day, too, and he was very, very tired when he finally reached the little cottage in the wood.

How pleased his parents were to see their son again! His mother hugged and kissed him, and then she put him straight to bed.

Tom stayed at home for several days, helping his father in the woods. When it was time to go back to court, Tom's mother made him a tiny umbrella from gossamer thread and, with Tom holding tightly to the handle, she blew it gently towards the royal palace.

But just as Tom floated down into the royal courtyard, the royal cook was passing by carrying a bowl of porridge for the king's breakfast. Down floated Tom, right in the centre of the bowl, splattering the cook from head to toe with sticky porridge.

"Oh, you naughty Tom Thumb!" she cried, and rushed off to complain about poor Tom to the king.

The king was very busy with the affairs of state that day, and so the cook put Tom in a mousetrap and kept him there for a whole week. When the king heard about the mousetrap, he felt so sorry for poor Tom that he granted him a royal pardon.

The king also gave both Tom and the cook a set of new clothes because their other garments had been ruined by the porridge. Tom looked so fine in his new clothes that the king made Tom a knight, despite his small size. The king knighted Tom with a silver darning needle which afterwards Sir Thomas used as his trusty sword.

One day Mab, Queen of the Fairies, came to the king's court to ask Tom to return to Fairyland with her for a visit. The Fairy Queen had watched over Tom since the day he was born and now she wanted to show him her kingdom. Tom was delighted to visit the home of the fairies, especially as they were all just as small as himself!

Tom stayed for four weeks, which was four *years* in mortal time, and when he returned he brought with him many fairy gifts. These included a jewelled sword and shield, a cloak of gold and an elegant pair of boots which would never wear out! The Fairy Queen also gave him a magic ring which she told him to rub in times of danger, and she would come to his aid.

The king and queen were delighted to see their tiny knight back again at court after such a long time. The king ordered the royal goldsmith to make a small golden table and chair which was then placed on the royal dining table so that Tom could eat at the royal table with the king and queen.

The king also gave Tom a tiny coach drawn by six small mice
so that he could travel in comfort when he visited his parents.
And so Tom Thumb, the king's small but very noble knight,
lived happily for many years, famed throughout the land for
his bravery, great charm and sharp wit.